EXTRA MOOSE MOSS
for HELEN

THIDWICK

The Big-Hearted Moose

Written
and illustrated by Dr. Seuss

RANDOM HOUSE NEW YORK

This title was originally catalogued by the Library of Congress as follows:
Thidwick, the big-hearted moose; written and illus. by Dr. Seuss [pseud.]   New York, Random House [1948]   I. Title.   PZ8.3.G276Th   48-8129
ISBN: 0-394-80086-9 (trade hardcover)   0-394-90086-3 (library binding)   0-394-84540-4 (trade paperback)

Manufactured in the United States of America

Upat Lake Winna-Bango . . . the far northern shore . . .
Lives a huge herd of moose, about sixty or more,
And they all go around in a big happy bunch
Looking for nice tender moose-moss to munch.

Up at Lake Winna-Bango, one day, they were lunching,
Just strolling along and enjoying their munching . . .
(For the moose-moss that day was especially fine) . . .
When it happened that Thidwick, the last moose in line,
Saw a Bingle Bug sitting.
The bug called out, "Hey!
It's *such* a long road
And it's *such* a hot day,
Would you mind if I rode
On your horns for a way?"

"Of course not!" smiled Thidwick, the Big-Hearted Moose.

"I'm happy my antlers can be of some use.

There's room there to spare, and I'm happy to share!

Be my guest and I hope that you're comfortable there!"

So the Bingle Bug picked out a nice easy seat

And the moose went on looking for moose-moss to eat.

Well . . .
An hour or so later
The bug heard a squeak,
And he heard the small voice
Of a Tree-Spider speak.
"I say!" said the spider,
"You've got a fine place!
That moose seems quite friendly,
Has such a nice face . . .
If I got on, *too,*
Do you think he would mind . . .?"

"Hop aboard!" laughed the bug. "And I think that you'll find
That the moose won't object. He's the big-hearted kind!"

"I accept," said the spider,
"With joy and delight."
And he started a web
On the horn to the right.

While the spider was spinning, he heard a gay song
And a fresh little Zinn-a-zu Bird came along.
He stopped. And he stared. And he chirped, "Well! *Well!* WELL!
What a smart place to build! What a great place to dwell!
I've been living on *trees* ever since I was born,
But here's something *new!* Why not live on a *horn!*
If there's room there for two, then there's room there for three!"

"There's plenty of room!"
Laughed the bug. "And it's free!"

Thidwick stopped walking.
What *was* all that talking?
These guests had caught Thidwick the Moose unawares.
"*Hey!*" he called out. "*What goes on there upstairs?*"

"Just building a nest, sir," the Zinn-a-zu said,
And began yanking hairs out of poor Thidwick's head.
And he plucked out exactly two hundred and four!
"Don't worry," he laughed. "You can always grow more!"

Then he dozed off to sleep in his fine moose-hair nest.
"This bird," murmured Thidwick, "is sort of a pest!
But I'm a good sport, so I'll just let him rest,
For a host, above all, must be nice to his guest."

"Besides, now, it's getting quite late in the day
And *surely* tomorrow they'll all go away."

But, alas! The next morning
The sun's early light
Brought to Thidwick's sad eyes
A most *un*welcome sight. . . .

"Meet my wife!" said the bird.
"I was married last night.

"And, perhaps, by the way,
I should mention to you
That her uncle is coming
To live with us, too.
You're a very fine host
So I knew you'd be willing . . ."

Then the Uncle, a Woodpecker,
Started in drilling!

All Thidwick's friends shouted, "GET RID OF THOSE PESTS!"
"I would, but I can't," sobbed poor Thidwick. *"They're guests!"*

"Guests indeed!" his friends answered, and all of them frowned.
"If *those* are your guests, we don't want *you* around!
You can't stay with us, 'cause you're just not our sort!"
And they all turned their backs and walked off with a snort.

Now the big friendless moose walked alone and forlorn,
With four great big woodpecker holes in his horn.

"What holes!" whispered Herman, a squirrel, who spied 'em.
"What holes to hide nuts in! *Hmmm!* Mind if I tried 'em?"

"They're yours!" called the woodpecker. "Get right inside 'em!
This big-hearted moose runs a public hotel!
Bring your nuts! Bring your wife! Bring your children as well!"

So the whole squirrel family all jumped on, pell mell.

And the very next thing the poor animal knew,
A Bobcat and Turtle were living there, too!
NOW what was the big-hearted moose going to do?

Well, what would YOU do
If it happened to YOU?

You couldn't say "Skat!" 'cause that wouldn't be right.
You couldn't shout "Scram!" 'cause that isn't polite.
A host has to put up with all kinds of pests,
For a host, above all, must be nice to his guests.
So you'd try hard to smile, and you'd try to look sweet
And you'd go right on looking for moose-moss to eat.

But now it was winter and *that* wasn't easy,
For moose-moss gets scarce when the weather gets freezy.
The food was soon gone on the cold northern shore
Of Lake Winna-Bango. There just was no more!
And all Thidwick's friends swam away in a bunch
To the south of the lake where there's moose-moss to munch.

He watched the herd leaving. And then Thidwick knew
He'd starve if he stayed here! He'd have to go, too!

He stepped in the water. Then, oh! what a fuss!
"STOP!" screamed his guests. "You can't do this to us!
These horns are our home and you've no right to take
Our home to the far distant side of the lake!"

"Be fair!" Thidwick begged, with a lump in his throat. . . .

"We're fair," said the bug.
"We'll decide this by vote.
All those in favor of going, say 'AYE,'
All those in favor of staying, say 'NAY'."

"AYE!" shouted Thidwick,
But when he was done . . .

"NAY!" they all yelled.
He lost 'leven to one.

"We win!" screamed the guests, "by a very large score!"
And poor, starving Thidwick climbed back on the shore.
Then, do you know what those pests did?
They asked in some more!

They asked in a fox, who jumped in from the trees,
They asked in some mice and they asked in some fleas.
They asked a big bear in and then, if you please,
Came a swarm of three hundred and sixty-two bees!

Poor Thidwick sank down, with a groan, to his knees.
And *then,* THEN came something that made his heart freeze.

Bullets came zinging right past Thidwick's face!
Guns were bang-binging all over the place!

"Get that moose!
Get that moose!"
Thidwick heard a voice call.
"Fire again and again
And shoot straight, one and all!
We *must* get his head
For the Harvard Club wall!"

Thidwick took to his heels with that load on his head!
With five hundred pounds on his horns, the moose fled!
He could have run faster without all those pests,
But a host, above all, must be nice to his guests.

Up canyon! Off cliff! Over wild rocky trail!
With bullets bang-bouncing around him like hail!
Up gully! Through gulch! And down slippery sluice,
With his hard-hearted guests raced the soft-hearted moose!

Then finally they had him!

Because of those pests, he had run out of luck,
Because of those guests on his horns, he was stuck!

He gasped! He felt faint! And the whole world grew fuzzy!
Thidwick was finished, completely. . . .

. . . *or WAS he* . . . ?

Finished . . . ?

Not Thidwick!

DECIDEDLY NOT!

It's true, he was in a most terrible spot,

But NOW he remembered a thing he'd forgot!

A wonderful something that happens each year

To the horns of all moose and the horns of all deer.

Today was the day,

Thidwick happened to know . . .

...that OLD horns come off so that NEW ones can grow!

And he called to the pests on his horns as he threw 'em,
"You wanted my horns; now you're quite welcome to 'em!
Keep 'em! They're yours!
As for ME, I shall take
Myself to the far distant
Side of the lake!"

And he swam Winna-Bango and found his old bunch,
And arrived just in time for a wonderful lunch
At the south of the lake, where there's moose-moss to munch.

His *old* horns today are
Where *you* knew they *would* be.
His guests are still on them,
All stuffed, as they *should* be.

BOOKS BY DR. SEUSS

And to Think That I Saw It on Mulberry Street
The 500 Hats of Bartholomew Cubbins
The King's Stilts
Horton Hatches the Egg
McElligot's Pool
Thidwick The Big-Hearted Moose
Bartholomew and the Oobleck
If I Ran the Zoo
Scrambled Eggs Super
Horton Hears a Who
On Beyond Zebra
If I Ran the Circus
How the Grinch Stole Christmas
Yertle the Turtle and Other Stories
Happy Birthday to You
The Sneetches and Other Stories
Dr. Seuss's Sleep Book
I Had Trouble in Getting to Solla Sollew
The Cat in the Hat Songbook
I Can Lick 30 Tigers Today and Other Stories
The Lorax
Did I Ever Tell You How Lucky You Are?
Hunches in Bunches
The Butter Battle Book

BEGINNER BOOKS

The Cat in the Hat
The Cat in the Hat Comes Back
One Fish Two Fish Red Fish Blue Fish
Green Eggs and Ham
Hop on Pop
Dr. Seuss's ABC
Fox in Socks
The Foot Book
My Book About Me
Mr. Brown Can Moo! Can You?
Marvin K. Mooney, Will You Please Go Now?
The Shape of Me and Other Stuff
There's A Wocket in My Pocket
Great Day for Up
Oh, The Thinks You Can Think
The Cat's Quizzer
I Can Read With My Eyes Shut
Oh Say Can You Say?